W9-BPJ-679

A Visit to the Farm

Daphne Ferrigan

Illustrated by Caroline Crossland

VIKING

This book is dedicated to Surrey Docks Farm

VIKING

Published by the Penguin Group
27 Wrights Lane, London W8 5TZ, England
Viking Penguin Inc., 40 West 23rd Street, New York, New York 10010, USA
Penguin Books Australia Ltd, Ringwood, Victoria, Australia
Penguin Books Canada Ltd, 2801 John Street, Markham, Ontario, Canada LR3 1B4
Penguin Books (NZ) Ltd, 182–190 Wairau Road, Auckland 10, New Zealand

Penguin Books Ltd, Registered Offices: Harmondsworth, Middlesex, England

First published 1990
1 3 5 7 9 10 8 6 4 2

Text copyright © Daphne Ferrigan, 1990
Illustrations copyright © Caroline Crossland, 1990

Filmset in Times by Chambers Wallace, London

Printed in Hong Kong

A CIP catalogue record for this book is available from the British Library

ISBN 0–670–82779–7

There are lots of animals to see and lots of things to do in a day at the farm.

Most farms keep dogs.

During the day the dogs help to look after the animals. They bark if the animals try to escape.

At night they sleep outside and chase the foxes away.

Inside the farmyard there are stables.
There is straw on the floor for the animals
to lie on.

stables

We've got a herd of goats,
sheep, cows, pigs, lots of hens,
ducks, geese, donkeys, horses,
bees, cats and dogs . . .

Outside the farmyard there are fields for the animals to run in. They also like to eat the grass. This is called grazing.

Here are the sheep.

The mother is called a ewe, the father is called a ram and the babies are called lambs.

Lambs and sheep are often kept for their meat. Sheep's meat is called mutton.

This lamb has lost its mother and needs to be fed by hand. Lambs drink milk until they are big enough to eat grass and hay. Hay is dried grass.

fleece

yarn

woollen
clothes

knitted jumper

In the winter sheep grow thick coats of wool. In the spring the farmer cuts the wool and it is made into yarn. Yarn is used for knitting or is made into cloth. Cutting the wool is called shearing. A coat of wool is called a fleece.

These goats are kept for milk. The mother makes milk to feed her babies.

The mother is called a nanny goat, the father is called a billy goat and the babies are called kids.

Some farms keep goats for meat.

Goats which give milk need extra food.
This food is a mixture of grains.

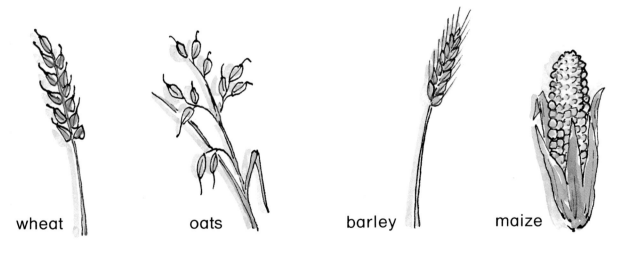

wheat   oats   barley   maize

Goats also like fruit, vegetables, tree bark
and lots of hay.

A farm which keeps cows for their milk is called a dairy farm.

Some farms keep sheep for their milk.

yoghurt

butter

cheese

ice-cream

cream

Yoghurt, cheese, butter, ice-cream and cream are all made from milk. Foods made from milk are called dairy products.

This cow will have a calf in the spring. It takes nine and a half months for a calf to grow inside its mother.

A mother is called a cow, a father is called a bull and a baby is called a calf.

A calf drinks milk until it is old enough to eat grass and hay. Then it will also need some grain.

calf

Dairy farms keep cows for milk but other farms keep them for meat. Cow's meat is called beef.

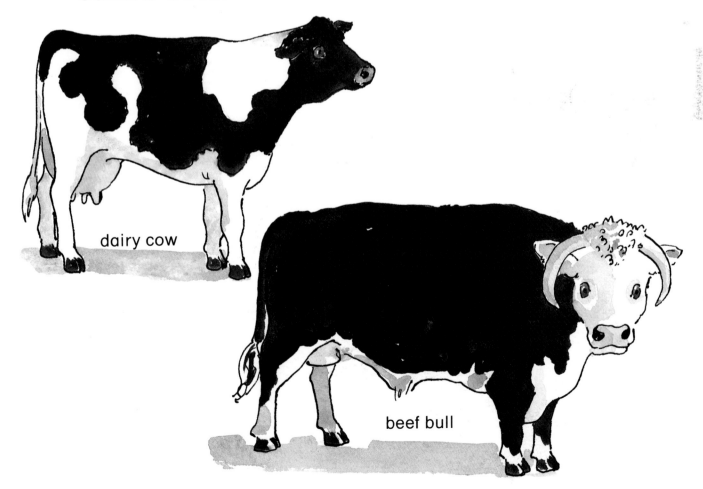

dairy cow

beef bull

These pigs live in a pigsty. Some farms have big sheds for pigs.

The mother pig is called a sow, the father is called a boar and the babies are called piglets.

Piglets drink their mother's milk. When they grow up they can eat most things, but farmers usually give them grain.

Pigs are only kept for meat. Pig's meat is called pork. Chops, bacon, ham and sausages are all made from pork.

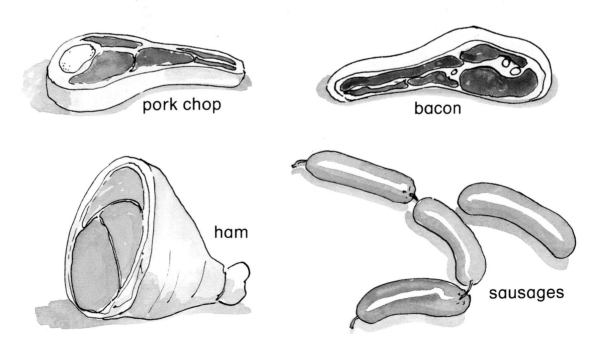

pork chop

bacon

ham

sausages

Here are the chickens.

The father is called a cockerel and the mother is called a hen. The baby bird is called a chick.

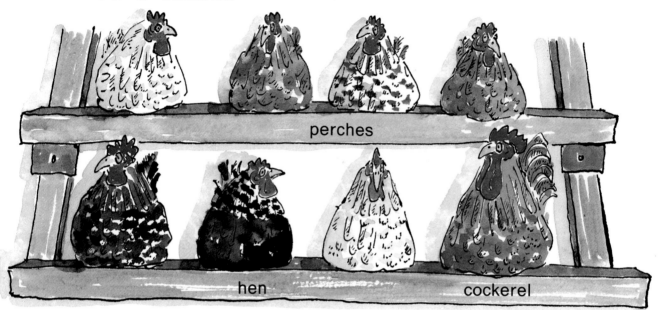

perches

hen

cockerel

These hens and cockerels live in a hen house. At night they sleep on perches. This is called roosting.

Do they peck?

Sometimes, but it doesn't hurt

During the day the hens lay eggs in nest boxes. The eggs are collected to eat.

Chickens can't fly very far but they like to run around. They scratch the ground looking for seeds and insects to eat. Some farmers give their chickens a food called layers' pellets.

chicks

This is the duck pond. The ducks swim here during the day. They graze underneath the trees. At night they sleep inside the duck house.

The mother duck lays eggs. She is called a duck. The father is called a drake and the babies are called ducklings.

Geese lay enormous eggs. They get angry when their eggs are collected.

The mother is called a goose and the father is called a gander. Baby geese are called goslings.

Geese like to graze in fields. They also eat grain.

Farmyard birds such as chickens, ducks and geese are called poultry. They are kept for their eggs and also for their meat.

HOW A CHICK IS BORN

Chicks grow inside eggs, but you won't find a chick inside an egg which you buy to eat.

A chick can only grow inside a special egg. It is called a fertile egg. A hen's egg is fertile after she has mated with a cockerel.

The egg has to be kept warm so that the chick can start to grow.

A hen usually sits on her eggs to keep them warm.

Some farmers keep eggs warm inside a special box. It is called an incubator.

After 21 days the chick is ready to hatch. It cracks the egg open with its beak.

A duckling takes 28 days to hatch. A gosling takes 30 days to hatch.

Donkeys are kept on farms all over the world. They are strong and can pull a cart or carry sacks on their backs.

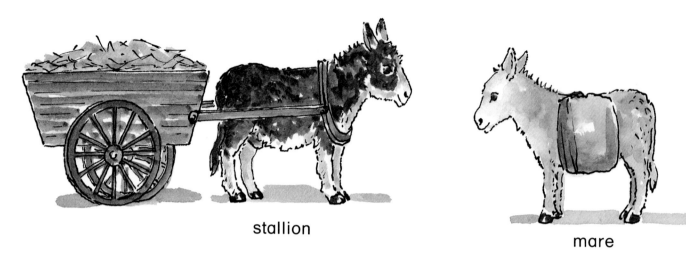

stallion

mare

A mother donkey is called a mare, a father is called a stallion and a baby is called a foal.

Today many farms have tractors and other machines to do the hard work.

Donkeys can be fun to ride.

They need to eat lots of hay and grass. If they work hard they can have some oats or bran.

Before tractors were invented, large farms used horses for heavy farm work. Horses are stronger and faster than donkeys.

Some horses are nearly 2 metres tall and they can weigh up to 1,000 kilograms.

A father horse is called a stallion and a mother horse is called a mare. The baby is called a foal.

mare

foal

stallion

A foal takes a long time to grow up. It drinks its mother's milk until it is six months old.

Grass is the most important food for horses. It is best if they can graze outside, but if they have to stay inside they need lots of hay to eat. Oats and bran are also fed to working horses.

Some farms keep bees.

In the spring and summer bees collect nectar and pollen from the flowers. They turn the nectar into honey and fill up the honeycombs in the hive ready for the winter.

There are three sorts of honey bee in every hive.

worker

Workers are female. They make the honey and look after the queen.

queen

The queen is female. She lays eggs. She can lay over 1,000 eggs in a day.

drone

Drones are male. They mate with the queen so that her eggs are fertile.

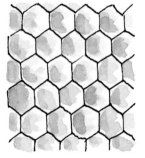
honeycomb

honey

Honey is taken out of the hives at the end of the summer. The beekeeper uses a machine to get the honey from the honeycomb. It is called an extractor.

extractor

Last of all, every farm needs a cat.

Cats chase the rats and mice out of the food store . . .

and pounce on wild birds who try to eat the grain.

A day on the farm is always busy.
Everyone needs a rest when all the work
is done.

GLOSSARY

beef	meat we get from cows
billy goat	male goat
boar	male pig
bran	rough powder left when grain is taken from flour
bull	male cow
calf	young cow
chick	young chicken
cockerel	male chicken
cow	female cow
dairy farm	farm which keeps animals for their milk
dairy product	food which is made from milk
drake	male duck
drone	male honey bee
duck	female duck
duckling	young duck
ewe	female sheep
extractor	machine used to get honey from a honeycomb
fertile egg	egg which can develop into a baby
fleece	coat which is cut from a sheep
foal	young horse or donkey
gander	male goose
goose	female goose
gosling	young goose
grain	small seed from plants such as wheat, oats and barley. Grain is used to feed animals.
graze	eat grass which is still growing
hatch	moment when a baby bird pushes itself out of an egg
hay	dry grass used to feed animals
hen	female chicken
honeycomb	place where honey bees store honey or eggs
incubator	box which keeps eggs warm so that baby birds can grow
kid	young goat
lamb	young sheep
layers' pellets	type of food for poultry
mare	female horse or donkey
mutton	meat we get from sheep
nanny	female goat
nectar	sweet juice made by flowers that bees make into honey
perches	strips of wood which hens rest and sleep on
piglet	young pig
pollen	yellow powder found in flowers
poultry	name for farmyard birds such as chickens, ducks and geese
queen bee	female honey bee which lays eggs
ram	male sheep
roost	way birds rest on a perch
shear	to cut wool from a sheep
sow	female pig
stable	building where animals shelter
stallion	male horse or donkey
straw	dried stems of plants such as wheat or oats. It is used for animal bedding.
tractor	machine used for heavy farm work
worker	female honey bee which makes honey and looks after queen bee
yarn	wool which has been made into thread